Little Red Caboose

Adapted by
Steve Metzger

Illustrated by Jill Dubin

- -

My First Hello Reader!
With Game Cards

- -

SCHOLASTIC INC.

New York Toronto London Auckland Sydney

Little Red Caboose goes
chug chug chug.

Hello, Family Members,

Learning to read is one of the most important accomplishments of early childhood. **Hello Reader!** books are designed to help children become skilled readers who like to read. Beginning readers learn to read by remembering frequently used words like "the," "is," and "and"; by using phonics skills to decode new words; and by interpreting picture and text clues. These books provide both the stories children enjoy and the structure they need to read fluently and independently. Here are suggestions for helping your child.

- Have your child think about a word he or she does not recognize right away. Provide hints such as "Let's see if we know the sounds" and "Have we read other words like this one?"
- Encourage your child to use phonics skills to sound out new words.
- Provide the word for your child when more assistance is needed so that he or she does not struggle and the experience of reading with you is a positive one.
- Encourage your child to have fun by reading with a lot of expression . . . like an actor!

I do hope that you and your child enjoy this book.

> —Francie Alexander
> Reading Specialist,
> Scholastic's Learning Ventures

Activity Pages
In the back of the book are skill-building activities. These are designed to give children further reading and comprehension practice and to provide added enjoyment. Offer help with directions as needed and encourage your child to have FUN with each activity.

Game Cards
In the middle of the book are eight pairs of game cards. These are designed to help your child become more familiar with words in the book and to play fun games.
• Have your child use the word cards to find matching words in the story. Then have him or her use the picture cards to find matching words in the story.
• Play a matching game. Here's how: Place the cards face up. Have your child match words to pictures. Once the child feels confident matching words to pictures, put cards face down. Have the child lift one card, then lift a second card to see if both match. If the cards match, the child can keep them. If not, place the cards face down once again.
Keep going until he or she finds all matches.

To Henry, for the smiles
— J. D.

Note: This text is an adaptation of a popular children's song.

No part of this publication may be reproduced, or stored in a retrieval system, or transmitted in any form or by any means, electronic, mechanical, photocopying, recording, or otherwise, without written permission of the publisher. For information regarding permissions, write to Scholastic Inc., Attention: Permissions Department, 555 Broadway, New York, NY 10012.

Library of Congress Cataloging-in-Publication Data
The Little Red Caboose / illustrated by Jill Dubin.
p. cm.— (My first hello reader!)
"Cartwheel books."
"With game cards."
Summary: Simple rhythmic text and illustrations describe the actions of the last car on a train. Includes related puzzles and activities.
ISBN 0-590-63598-0
[1. Railroads—Trains—Fiction.] I. Dubin, Jill, Ill. II. Series.
PZ7.L73535 1998
[E]—dc21
98-24330
CIP
AC

10 9 8 7 6 5 4

9/9 0/0 01 02 03

Printed in the U.S.A.

24

First printing, November 1998

Little Red Caboose goes
chug chug chug.

Little Red Caboose is
behind the train.

A smokestack is on
its back.

It's chugging down
the track.

Little Red Caboose is
behind the train.

Little Red Caboose goes
chug chug chug.

Little Red Caboose goes
chug chug chug.

Little Red Caboose
moves very fast.

It watches trees go by.

It watches birds that fly.

Little Red Caboose
moves very fast.

Little Red Caboose goes
chug chug chug.

Little Red Caboose goes
chug chug chug.

Little Red Caboose
moves through the dark.

It sees the stars at night.
It sees the moon so bright.

Little Red Caboose
moves through the dark.

Little Red Caboose goes
chug chug chug.

Little Red Caboose goes
chug chug chug.

Little Red Caboose is
behind the train.

It's hanging on the end.
It's coming round the bend.

Little Red Caboose is
behind the train.

Rebus Picture Puzzle

Can you recognize these words from the story?

t + = ?

fl + = ?

+ es = ?

Opposites

Opposites are words that mean something completely different. For example, **good** is the opposite of **bad**.

Draw a line to match each word with its opposite.

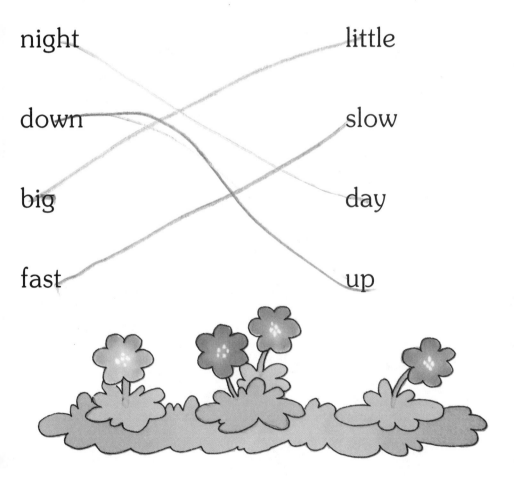

night   little

down   slow

big   day

fast   up

I Spy

Circle the things you might *see* *only* at night.

Train Maze

Help the train to get back to the station.

Rhyme Time

Moon and **spoon** are two words that rhyme.
In each row point to the picture that rhymes with
each word.

sees

very

back

at

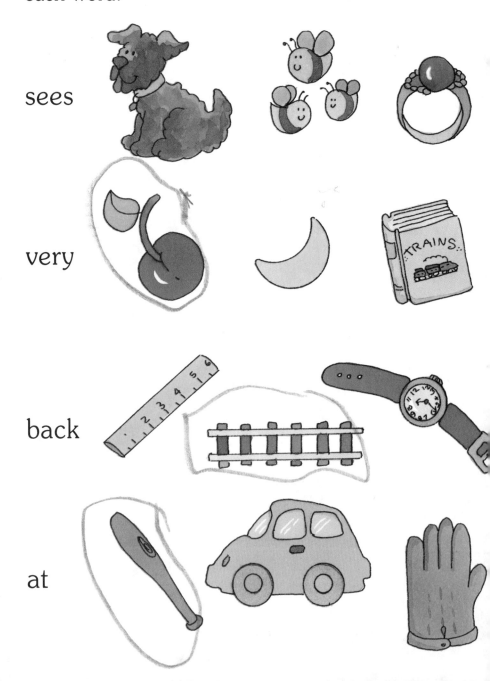

Train Trip

Which of these things would you find in or on a train?

ANSWERS

Rebus Picture Puzzle

t + 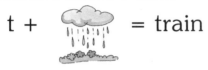 = train

fl + 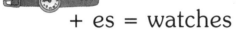 = fly

 + es = watches

Opposites

night ⟍ little
down ⤬ slow
big ⤬ day
fast up

I Spy

Train Maze

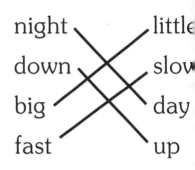

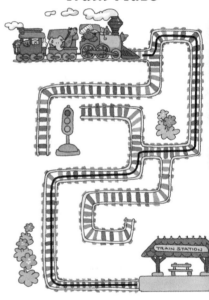

Rhyme Time

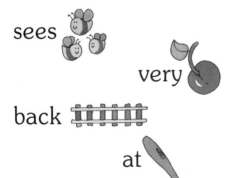

sees

very

back

at

Train Trip

These are the things you woul find in or on a train.